Dear Parents and Educators,

Welcome to Penguin Young Readers! As parents and educators, you know that each child develops at his or her own pace—in terms of speech, critical thinking, and, of course, reading. Penguin Young Readers recognizes this fact. As a result, each Penguin Young Readers book is assigned a traditional easy-to-read level (1–4) as well as a Guided Reading Level (A–P). Both of these systems will help you choose the right book for your child. Please refer to the back of each book for specific leveling information. Penguin Young Readers features esteemed authors and illustrators, stories about favorite characters, fascinating nonfiction, and more!

The Gingerbread Kid Goes to School

LEVEL 2

GUIDED READING LEVEL G

This book is perfect for a **Progressing Reader** who:

- can figure out unknown words by using picture and context clues;
- can recognize beginning, middle, and ending sounds;
- can make and confirm predictions about what will happen in the text; and
- can distinguish between fiction and nonfiction.

Here are some **activities** you can do during and after reading this book:

- Cause and Effect: Cause and effect is when you do something and it makes something happen. The effect is *what* happened and the cause is *why* it happened. In this story, there are many examples of cause and effect. One example is when the principal put the eyes on the gingerbread kid (cause) and he springs to life (effect). Reread the story and discuss the instances of cause and effect.
- Creative Writing: At the end of the story, the boy's dog eats the gingerbread kid. This ending is a funny surprise, but there are lots of other possible endings. On a separate sheet of paper, write another funny ending for this story.

Remember, sharing the love of reading with a child is the best gift you can give!

—Bonnie Bader, EdM
Penguin Young Readers program

*Penguin Young Readers are leveled by independent reviewers applying the standards developed by Irene Fountas and Gay Su Pinnell in *Matching Books to Readers: Using Leveled Books in Guided Reading*, Heinemann, 1999.

For Amanda, Jessica, and Katie,
who live across the street—JH

To Kumari—DP

ISBN 978-0-545-52374-5

18 17 17/0

Printed in the U.S.A. 40

First Scholastic printing, December 2012

The Gingerbread Kid Goes to School

by Joan Holub
illustrated by Debbie Palen

SCHOLASTIC INC.

One day, the principal
baked a gingerbread kid.
He took it
in his lunch box.

Oh no!

Something was missing!

The principal put on

two candy eyes.

Suddenly,
the gingerbread
kid winked.

He did a flip
off the desk.

He did a cartwheel
on the floor.
Then he ran away.

"Come back!" shouted the principal.

The principal ran after the gingerbread kid.

The gingerbread kid

laughed and shouted,

“I’m the gingerbread kid.

I’m fast as can be.

You can run, run, run.

But you can’t catch me!”

The gingerbread kid ran
to the playground.

He kicked a ball

over the fence.

“Come back!”

shouted two gym coaches.

Then they ran after him.

The gingerbread kid
laughed and shouted,
"I'm the gingerbread kid.
I'm fast as can be.
You can run, run, run.
But you can't catch me!"

The gingerbread kid ran

into the lunchroom.

He hopped in
the beans
and the rice.

"Come back!"

shouted the three lunch ladies.

They dropped their spoons

and ran after him.

The gingerbread kid

laughed and shouted,

“I’m the gingerbread kid.

I’m fast as can be.

You can run, run, run.

But you can’t catch me!”

The gingerbread kid ran by
four teachers in the hall.

He spilled their

jars of paint.

“Come back!” they shouted.

Then they ran after him.

The gingerbread kid

laughed and shouted,

“I’m the gingerbread kid.

I’m fast as can be.

You can run, run, run.

But you can’t catch me!”

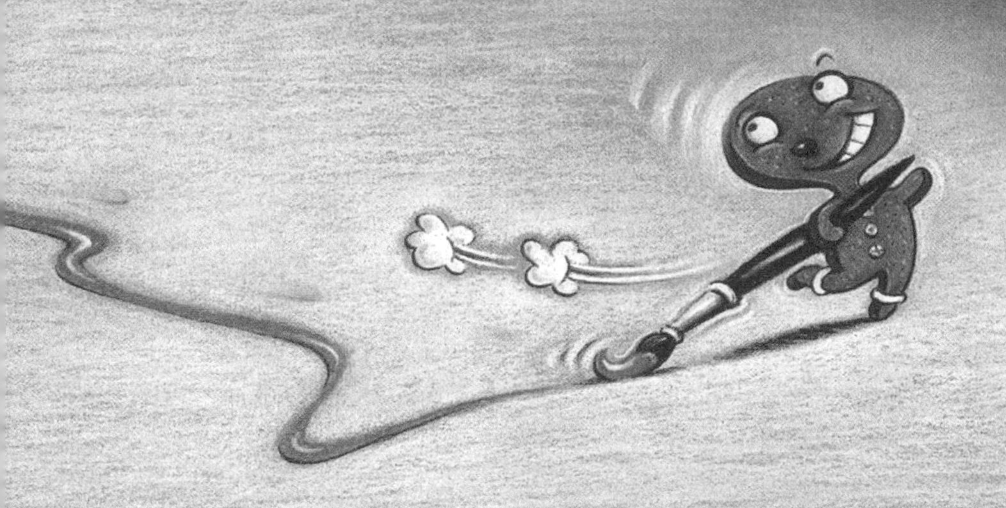

The gingerbread kid ran
into the library.
He jumped on a boy's desk.

"Chase me,"

said the gingerbread kid.

The boy kept reading.

"CHASE ME!"

shouted the gingerbread kid.

The boy shook his head.

"What kind of kid wants to read?"

asked the gingerbread kid.

"A smart kid,"

said the boy.

“Not as smart as me,”

said the gingerbread kid.

“I ran away from the principal,

two gym coaches,

three lunch ladies,

and four teachers.

I can run away from you, too!”

"No, you can't," said the boy.

"Here are five reasons why."

The boy made a fist.

One by one,

he held up his fingers.

“One.

Two.

Three.

Four.

FIVE.”

Then he grabbed
the gingerbread kid.
"Gotcha!" the boy said.

Like magic,

the gingerbread kid

turned into a cookie again.

Suddenly,

everyone ran into the library.

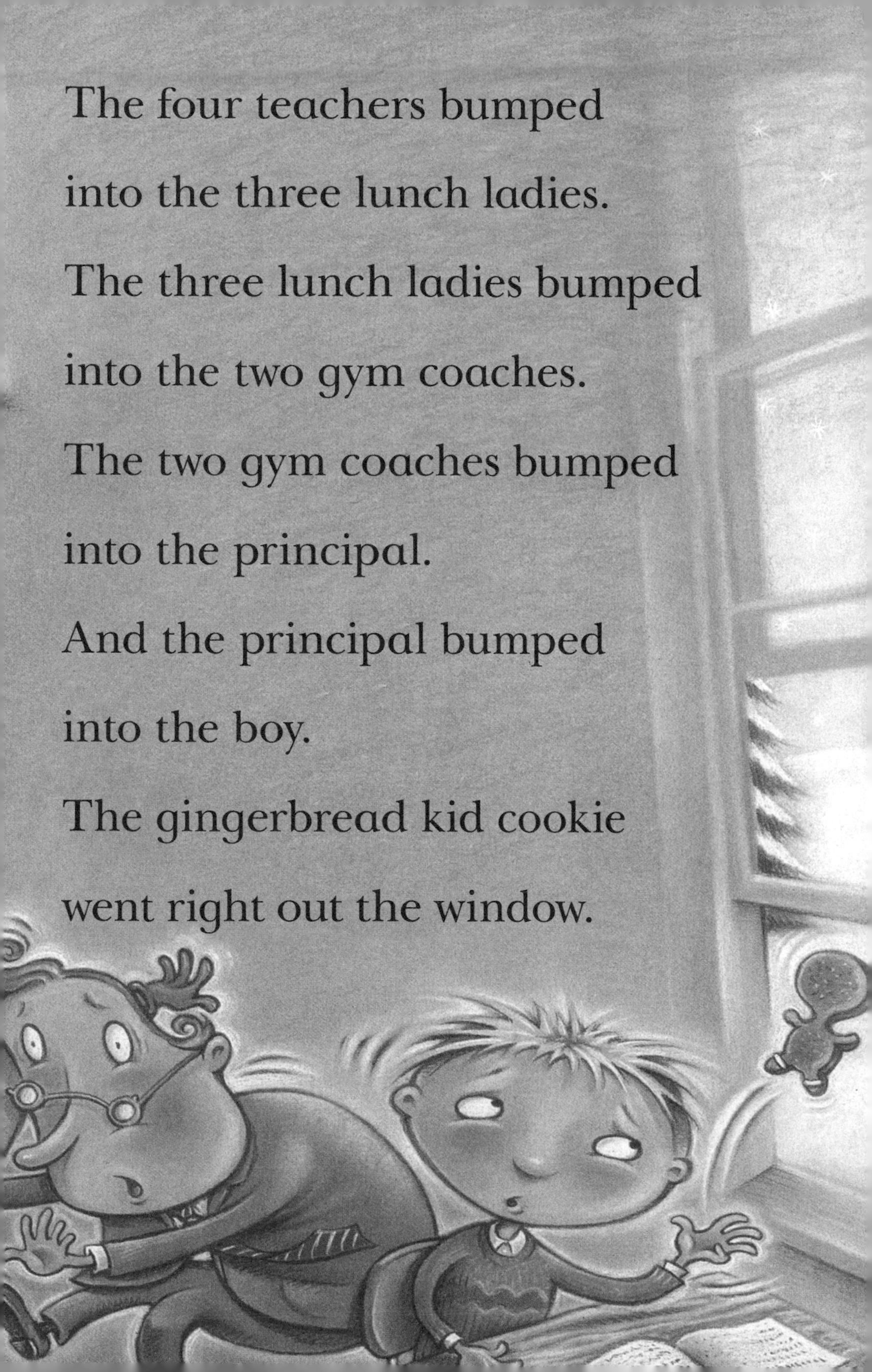

The four teachers bumped

into the three lunch ladies.

The three lunch ladies bumped

into the two gym coaches.

The two gym coaches bumped

into the principal.

And the principal bumped

into the boy.

The gingerbread kid cookie

went right out the window.

And right outside,

the smart boy's smart dog

was waiting.

Chomp!

Chomp!